HOPSCOTCH FAIRY TALES

The Three Little Pigs

by Anne Walter and Daniel Postgate

W
FRANKLIN WATTS
LONDON•SYDNEY

Once upon a time, there
were three little pigs.

One day, their mother said, "You're old enough to build your own houses now. But beware of the big bad wolf!"

Soon the three little pigs
met a man carrying straw.
"Please may I have some straw?"
asked the first little pig.
"Yes," replied the man.

The first little pig quickly built
a house of straw.

Next, they met a man carrying sticks. "Please may I have some sticks?" asked the second little pig. "Of course," replied the man.

The second little pig quickly built a house of sticks.

Then the third little pig met a
man carrying bricks. "Please may
I have some bricks?" he asked.
"Certainly," replied the man.

The third little pig worked all week long on his house of bricks.

The big bad wolf soon knocked
at the first little pig's door.
"Little pig, little pig, let me in!"
he called.

The first little pig remembered
what his mother had told him.
"Not by the hairs on my chinny
chin chin!" he replied.

"Then I'll huff and I'll puff and I'll blow your house in!" roared the wolf. He huffed and he puffed and he blew the straw house down.

The first little pig fled to his brother's house.

The big bad wolf knocked at the second little pig's door. "Little pig, little pig, let me in!" he called.

"Not by the hairs on my chinny chin chin!" replied the second little pig, shaking.

"Then I'll huff and I'll puff and I'll blow your house in!" roared the wolf. He huffed and he puffed and he blew the stick house down.

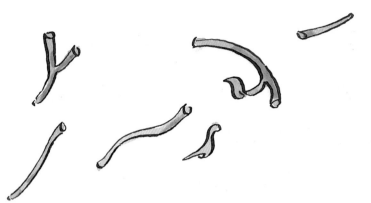

The two little pigs fled
to their brother's house.

The big bad wolf knocked at the third little pig's door. "Little pig, little pig, let me in!" he called.

"Not by the hairs on my chinny chin chin!" came the reply.

"Then I'll huff and I'll puff and I'll blow your house in!" roared the wolf again.

"Just you try it!" called the third
little pig, cheekily.

The wolf huffed and he puffed …

and he huffed and he puffed …

but he could not blow that brick

house down.

The wolf was very angry.
He decided to climb onto the
roof and down the chimney
to get his dinner.

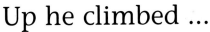 Up he climbed ...

in he squeezed ...

and down he
dropped ...

… straight into the third little pig's cooking pot!

The wolf was never seen again!
The three little pigs celebrated
with a big party.

POP!

Hopscotch has been specially designed to fit the requirements of the Literacy Framework. It offers real books by top authors and illustrators for children developing their reading skills. There are 55 Hopscotch stories to choose from:

* hardback